# I Am Your Hamster

This is my book. I will teach you how to care for me after you bring me home. You will find more facts about me in these bubbles throughout the book.

# I Am Your Hamster

By Gill Page

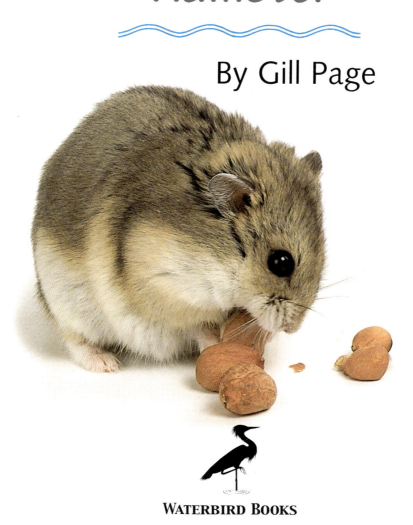

**WATERBIRD BOOKS**

# The Author

Gill Page has been involved with a wide variety of animals for many years. She has run a successful pet center and has helped rescue and find homes for unwanted animals. She has cared for many animals of her own and is eager to pass on her experience so that children may learn how to care for their pets lovingly and responsibly.

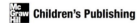 **Children's Publishing**

This edition published in the
United States of America in 2004 by
Waterbird Books
an imprint of McGraw-Hill Children's Publishing,
a Division of The McGraw-Hill Companies
8787 Orion Place
Columbus, Ohio 43240-4027

www.MHkids.com

Library of Congress Cataloging-in-Publication Data is on file with the publisher.

© 2000 Interpet Publishing Ltd.
All rights reserved.

All rights reserved. Except as permitted under the United States Copyright Act, no part of this publication may be reproduced or distributed in any form or by any means, or stored in a database retrieval system, without prior written permission from the publisher.

Printed in Hong Kong.

ISBN 0-7696-3389-7

1 2 3 4 5 6 7 8 9 10 IPP 09 08 07 06 05 04 03

**Credits**

*Editor:* Philip de Ste. Croix
*Designer:* Phil Clucas MSIAD
*U.S. Editors:* Joanna Callihan and
 Catherine Stewart
*Production Editor:* Lowell Gilbert
*Studio photography:* Neil Sutherland
*Colour artwork:* Rod Ferring
*Production management:* Consortium,
 Poslingford, Suffolk CO10 8RA

# Contents

| | |
|---|---|
| Making Friends | 6 |
| Getting to Know Me | 8 |
| Taking Me Home | 10 |
| Getting Settled | 12 |
| My Own Cage | 14 |
| Time for Bed | 16 |
| My Favorite Foods | 18 |
| Good Food, Bad Food | 20 |
| Meal Times | 22 |
| Feeding Schedule | 23 |
| Treats and Tidbits | 24 |
| Living on My Own | 26 |
| Toys and Playtime | 28 |
| Looking My Best | 30 |
| Playing Indoors | 32 |
| Visits to My Doctor | 34 |
| If I Have Babies | 36 |
| How to Write a Report on Your Pet | 38 |
| Hamster Checklist | 39 |
| I Am a Syrian Hamster | 40 |
| I Am a Russian Dwarf Hamster | 42 |
| I Am a Chinese Hamster | 44 |
| A Note to Parents | 46 |
| Acknowledgements | 48 |

# Making Friends

Hello. I am your new friend. What is your name? You can give me a short name, and then I will know when you are calling me. I want a home of my own that is safe and cozy. I will take a little time to get used to you, and then we will be very good friends.

*I am a fast runner and like to escape from my cage if you don't shut it properly.*

*I am very curious, and I love to explore wherever I go.*

I have thick, soft hair and shiny, black eyes. I keep myself very clean, but you can also help by brushing me. I like my home to be clean and tidy. I want to live on my own. I do not like sharing my house with anybody else. I like fresh food and water every day. I sleep in the daytime and play at night. I may be very small, but I am very brave. My favorite game is escaping from my cage! I may be tiny but I need lots of exercise. If I lived in the wild, I would run and run for miles every night. I can have long or short hair, which can grow in many different colors.

# Getting to Know Me

I am tiny, but very quick. When I first come to live with you, I will weigh about 3 ounces (90 grams). My fur is usually short and shiny. Some of my friends have really long hair, but they are much harder to care for than I am. They have to be brushed every day. I can be all one color, mostly a golden brown with a white tummy, or a mixture of colors. I am called a Syrian, or Golden, hamster. You can buy two other kinds of hamsters. One is a Chinese hamster. He looks a bit like a mouse. The other is the Russian hamster. He is small, fluffy and round. I'll tell you more about them at the end of this book.

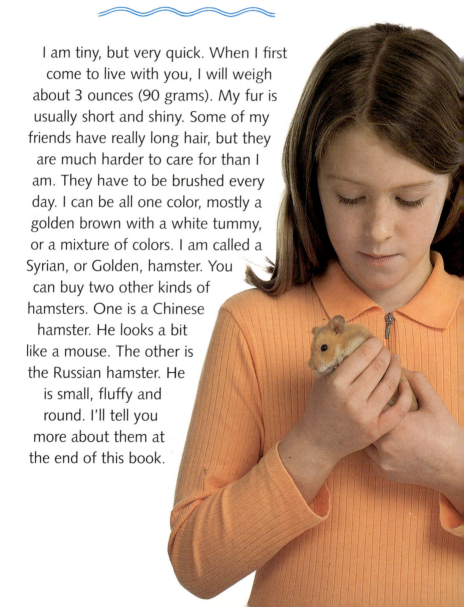

*I am a Russian hamster, and I am smaller than my Syrian relative.*

I have four toes on both of my front feet and five on both of my back feet. My teeth keep growing all the time. I must have lots of things to chew on to keep them short. Please pick me up carefully. If you grab me and lift me up quickly, it feels as if a big monster has swooped down and carried me away. That really scares me. Slide one hand under me, and cup the other hand around the front of my body. Hold me gently close to you. Please don't drop me.

I have five toes on my back feet.

But only four toes on my front feet.

## Taking Me Home

Buy me from a pet shop or a breeder. Sometimes animal shelters have a few of us that need good homes. I must be five weeks old before you may take me home. If you have never had a friend like me before, it is best to choose a hamster with short hair. We are much easier to care for than long-haired hamsters. I should have a shiny coat with no bald patches. I should not have insects in my fur. My eyes should be bright and shiny, and my nose should be clean.

The most important place to look is under my little tail. The fur here must be dry. If it is wet, do not buy me. I have a disease called "wet tail" and I may die. Since I will be living on my own, you can choose either a boy or a girl. We will fight each other if we are kept in the same cage. A pet case with bedding in the bottom will keep me safe on the journey home. Put me into my new house, with food and water, when we get home.

*I am so happy you have chosen me. Put me into the case for the journey home.*

# Getting Settled

I will be frightened for a while when I first get home. I will probably hide in my bedding. I sleep all day and wake up in the evening. When I think that nobody is looking, I will sneak out to explore. I will look around my cage and eat some food and drink some water. When I am still settling in, just feed me, give me water, and keep the cage clean. Don't try to pick me up for a while. I may try and bite you if I think you are going to hurt me. I have to learn to trust you. When I do, I will happily let you pick me up.

*Once I have grown to trust you, we will become friends.*

Daytime is my bedtime. Just like you, I can be grumpy if someone wakes me up. After about two weeks, you can start to make friends with me. Stroke me with one finger. Later, put a treat in your hand and stretch your hand into my cage. I might sit on your hand and try to taste you with my teeth. Keep very still and I will not bite. If I stand on my back legs and make a noise, I am still scared. Keep trying. I'm sure we'll soon be friends.

# My Own Cage

I will spend most of the time in my cage, so please buy me a nice, big one. I will always be trying to escape, so make sure the cage is made for hamsters. I am awake all night, so I need lots of room to run around and play while you are asleep. Most of the cages you can buy are made of wire with a plastic base. You can also buy a cage that allows you to add tunnels and rooms.

*A box within my cage makes an ideal nest site for me.*

A large fish tank can be made into a nice home for me. It will need a wire top clipped onto it. The tank must not be too deep, though. If it is, it will get too hot and stuffy inside and will make me sick. I need a room to sleep in.

I just love making nests and digging tunnels. If I am bored, I will try to escape. My home must be kept inside your house and set high off the floor. I cannot live outside. If I get cold, I may die.

## Time for Bed

There are all sorts of things you can use for my bedding. I don't sleep with sheets and blankets like you do. I like wood chips. I can eat them and sleep on them, too. I can burrow into them when I am scared. Bedding that is made just for me is fun. You can buy paper bedding or fluffy, soft stuff. I will make a cozy little nest with this.

*I like my nest to be snuggly and warm*

Shredded paper

Nestle down

Wood shavings

Wool fiber

Put wood shavings in the bottom of my house. They will soak up the moisture. Everyday, you will need to throw out the dirty shavings and any old pieces of food that I have not eaten. If you don't, my cage will get very smelly. Then, add more clean bedding. At the end of the week, put me into my carrying case. This will keep me safe while you are cleaning my house. Clear out all the bedding. Wipe out the cage with a damp cloth, or use cage wipes to make it smell sweet. Make sure the cage is dry before you put me and my bedding back in.

*I like to nibble on nuts. They are good for my teeth, too.*

## My Favorite Foods

Before you bring me home, ask about the food I have been eating. It is often a mixture that comes in a box. Buy some of the same food to take home with me. Also ask if I have been allowed to eat fresh food. If I haven't, just give me a little bit to start with. I can have a little more each day, as long as it doesn't upset my stomach. A good diet for me is hamster food along with extra fruit, nuts, and vegetables.

Sprout tops

Vitamin drops

Hay

Hamster mix

Apple

Carrot

Parsnip

I like my food to be clean and fresh. When I eat, I push as much I can into my mouth. Inside, at each side of my mouth, I have a pocket, called a pouch. I know it makes me look funny and chubby-cheeked, but it is my way of carrying food back to my nest.

Some of the fresh foods I can eat are apples, pears, carrots, and tomatoes. In the summer, you can pick wild plants for me. Dandelion and clover are good choices. Once or twice a week you can give me a tiny piece of hard cheese or even one or two mealworms, which you can buy from a pet shop.

# Good Food, Bad Food

I must tell you about a few of the things I must not eat. Some of them will make me very sick. Never, ever, give me bracken, ragwort, buttercup, or tomato leaves. Before you feed me anything, ask your mom or dad to check it out. There are a lot of weeds and fresh grass that I can eat, but I don't like the smell or taste of the plants growing next to a road. I think the fumes from all the cars that drive by make it taste funny.

You will need to wash the food before you give it to me. There are a few fruits and vegetables that will give me a stomach ache. I should not eat raw potatoes, leeks, white cabbage, oranges, and kiwi fruit. I must not have too much lettuce or cucumber, either. I like nibbling on nuts, but I can not eat horse chestnuts. They are bad for me.

# Meal Times

I like small, heavy dishes for my food. I need one dish for the dry food and one dish for my fruit and vegetables. If my dish is too big, I will walk all over my food. A dish that is made of pottery is easy to keep clean. I may chew up a plastic dish. I like to drink clean water every day. When I eat wood shavings, I get very thirsty. A water bottle lets me have a drink any time I need one. The water stays clean in a bottle, but if it is in a dish, I may stand in it and make it dirty. Change the water daily, and wash the bottle every week.

*I will need two heavy bowls and a drinking bottle for fresh water.*

## Feeding Schedule

I like to have my meals at the same time every day. I will know if you are late feeding me! You can leave my dry food in the cage all day. Then, I can nibble at my food when I feel hungry. Feed me in the morning and evening. I have a very small stomach. I only need about two, heaping teaspoonfuls of dry food. I always store my food, so you will soon see if you are giving me too much.

### Breakfast
A little bit of hamster mix.

### Dinner
Top off the hamster mix in my bowl. Give me some fresh fruit or vegetables, and throw out any fruit or veggies left over from the day before. Check the water bottle.

Mineral wheel

Alfalfa squares

Seed treat

Wood chews

Sunflower seeds

*I can have one of these treats every day. The banana-flavored wood chews are for me to gnaw. The mineral wheel must stay in my cage.*

# Treats and Tidbits

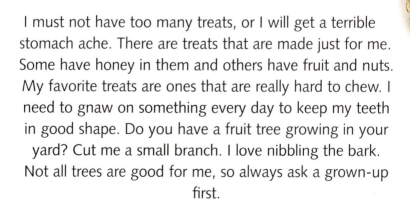

I must not have too many treats, or I will get a terrible stomach ache. There are treats that are made just for me. Some have honey in them and others have fruit and nuts. My favorite treats are ones that are really hard to chew. I need to gnaw on something every day to keep my teeth in good shape. Do you have a fruit tree growing in your yard? Cut me a small branch. I love nibbling the bark. Not all trees are good for me, so always ask a grown-up first.

*I am going to hide some of this to eat later.*

You can also buy wood chews for me. If I don't have things to gnaw, my teeth will get so long that I will not be able to eat at all. You can hang a treat called *spray millet* in my cage. People buy it for their pet birds, but I like it, too. Pet shops sell mineral wheels for me. Please hang one in my cage, and then I can nibble it whenever I need to. Remember to add pet vitamin drops to my food twice a week.

# Living on My Own

I don't like living with other hamsters. I only like living by myself. I know just how I want my home to be. I like to have my nest and my food bowl to myself. I love storing my food in my nest. Then, if I wake up and feel hungry, I can have a quick snack, and I will not have to move far. I don't want to find anyone else eating *my* food. I know where my water bottle is, and nobody else must use it.

My eyes are bright and shiny, but I can only see things that are close to my nose, so I get scared when something, like another hamster, appears in front of me. That is when I may bite. If I am put with another hamster, we will fight, and we may hurt each other badly. Also, you should never leave me alone with your pet cat or dog. They will see me as a tasty snack.

*Please try to make my home interesting. I enjoy climbing over logs, exploring cardboard tunnels, or simply running around in wood shavings.*

# Toys and Playtime

I may not want to play when I first come to live with you, but as soon as I learn that you will not hurt me, we can play together. You can buy toys for me from the pet shop. A wheel in my cage will make me think I am running a long way. When I am awake, I rush around my cage looking for things to do. If you make me a mini-playground, I will have hours of fun playing in it.

*You must not leave me in a plastic ball for too long, or I will get tired.*

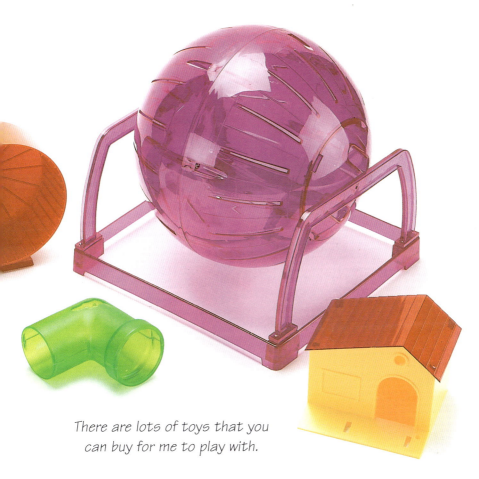

*There are lots of toys that you can buy for me to play with.*

I like to hide in things and I love running through tunnels. A toilet paper roll makes a great tunnel. Push one end of the tube into the shavings. I can pretend I am in a burrow under the ground. Hollow plastic balls can make me tired very quickly. I like playing in the early morning or in the evening. We will have just enough time for a game before you go to school. We can play again when you get home.

# Looking My Best

I spend a lot of time keeping my fur clean and shiny. You can help by brushing my hair. Use a soft brush. I can reach nearly every part of my body with my teeth, so I do not need brushing every day. I never, ever, need a bath. If I do get a little grubby, just wipe my fur with a damp cloth. One way to tell if I am upset about something is to watch me. I will clean and clean my fur if I am annoyed.

Don't brush too hard.

You do not have to buy me a big brush. A little one is fine. You can even use a soft, dry toothbrush. Please brush me gently. You might make my skin sore if you brush me too hard. Start at my head, and brush my fur the same way as it grows. Furry hamsters need brushing every day. You will have to buy a comb for them, too. Hamsters don't need to brush their teeth. We keep our teeth clean by chewing things. A raw carrot is a great tooth-cleaner. An apple is also good for our teeth.

*Brush me only in the direction in which my fur grows—from my head toward my tail.*

# Playing Indoors

I need lots of exercise. I get bored in my cage if there's not much to do. If I am really tame, you may consider letting me play outside my cage. First, check the room where I am going to run free. Is it safe for me? I am so tiny and I can run so fast that if I hide, you will not be able to see where I am. I can squeeze into tiny cracks. I may even get stuck. I sometimes chew my way into sofas or even into your bed.

I am a super climber. I can climb high up the curtains, but I am not very good at getting down again. Can you rescue me? Your bedroom may be the best place to play. Put a notice on the outside of the door that says, "Hamster Loose." Then, nobody will open the door and let me out. If I escape, you will have to make a trap to catch me. Put some bedding and food in the bottom of a bucket. Make a staircase from books next to it. If I climb up and get into the bucket, I will not be able to climb out again, and you can rescue me.

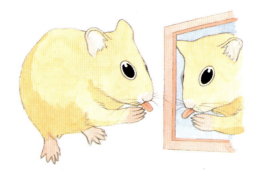

# Visits to My Doctor

My doctor is called a *veterinarian* or *vet* for short. He or she will take care of me if I am sick. When I am ill, you must get me to the vet quickly. If I am scratching, the vet will be able to tell you why I am so itchy. I may have fleas, lice, or mites. The vet will give you something to put on my fur to make me feel better.

*Feel my body for lumps or bumps. If you find any, take me to the vet.*

There are other times when you should take me to the vet. I must go if I have a runny nose or watery eyes. I must go if I make a wheezy noise when I breathe. Each week, you should feel my body for lumps and bumps. Take me to the vet if my droppings are runny or if the fur under my tail is always wet. If my teeth or claws grow too long, the vet can cut them for me. I don't like when the vet trims my feet and claws, but I always feel a lot better when it has been done. I am very lucky because I do not need to have injections every year to keep me safe from disease.

# If I Have Babies

I do not want to have babies. Looking after them is very hard work for you and me. If I do, I need a quiet place to care for my babies. I will need a lot of extra bedding so I can build a bigger nest. I will probably have between five and seven babies, or even more.

*My mom carried me inside of her for 16 days.*

My babies are born without any fur, and their eyes are closed tight. I will feed them my milk for about three weeks. Please feed me extra food so that I can make a lot of milk. When the babies are tiny, do not try to touch them or me. I will think they are in danger and I may even kill them. Let the babies live with me until they are 25 days old. I will show them how to eat solid food. Then, put each one into its own cage. The vet can tell you which ones are boys and which are girls. After that, you can let them go live with some new friends.

# How to Write a Report on Your Pet

You may choose to write a report about your pet for school. Start by making an outline of what you would like to say about your pet. The outline should begin with an introduction and end with a conclusion. In between the introduction and the conclusion, you should list three or four characteristics about your pet that you would like to write about.

In the introduction, state your topic, which is your pet, and tell the reader what you will be discussing in the rest of your report.

After the introduction, provide the reader with a more detailed description of your pet's characteristics. For instance, you may want to talk about your pet's appearance, your pet's favorite toys, and your pet's quirky mannerisms. Cover these topics in separate paragraphs in your report.

After you finish the detailed description of your pet's characteristics, you should give a short summary of your whole report. Then, you may want to end your report with a funny story about your pet. When you are finished, you will have a wonderful record of your pet that you can return to in years to come.

# Hamster Checklist

1. Give me food and water every day.
2. Wash my food bowls every day.
3. Check that my eyes and ears are clean everyday.
4. Check if I empty the food out of my pouches everyday.
5. Check that my fur and skin are clean, everyday.
6. Check my teeth every week.
7. Clean my cage thoroughly every week.
8. Check my body for lumps and bumps every week.
9. See that my claws are short and do not have splits.
10. Make sure that I am eating my food.

# I Am a Syrian Hamster

I have short hair. The color of my fur is golden-brown. I have a white tummy and little white patches of fur on my face. Other hamsters that have a coat of all one color are called self-colored. Some hamsters have pale, cream-colored fur. If I have white hair and pink eyes, I am an *albino*. Some hamsters have colored fur with patches of white in it. These hamsters are called *piebald*. Tortoiseshell hamsters have fur that is brown, yellow, and red, and they are always girls. Some hamsters have very shiny fur, and they are called *satin* hamsters.

My friends that have soft, fluffy hair are called *long-haired* or *teddy bear* hamsters. This sort of fur needs to be brushed every day to keep it neat and clean. Brushing the fur keeps it from getting messy and tangled.

A white stripe of fur around my middle is called a band.

# I Am a Russian Dwarf Hamster

I am a very small, round hamster. I am only about 4 inches (10cm) long, even when I am fully grown. My fur is a little bit longer than a Syrian's. I look like a little ball of fluff. My hair is mostly gray. The fur on my tummy is white or a lighter gray. I often have a dark stripe of fur. It goes from the tip of my nose, along my back, and down to my little tail. I have white fur around my mouth and cheeks.

I am a bit easier to tame than my bigger relatives. If you buy two baby brothers, we can live together in a large cage. We need our own areas of the cage to live in, though. I can have my nest at one end of our house, and my brother can live at the other end. You can have two sisters living together, but they fight more than boys, and can hurt each other. I do not want to have babies. But, if I have them, there will be four or five of them. I can live a bit longer than other hamsters.

*Please cup me in your hands to pick me up.*

# I Am a Chinese Hamster

I am another small hamster. I grow to be about 5 inches (12.5cm) long. I have a longer tail than other hamsters. I can curl my tail round your finger so that I won't fall off of your hand. I look a little bit like a mouse, but I am not a mouse! My fur is short and smooth. It is a gray–brown color. I have white hair on my tummy. There is a strip of black fur that starts on the top of my head, runs along my back, and ends at the top of my tail. I have small ears. They may have a tiny bit of black hair on the tips.

I use my whiskers to feel for things in the dark.

I have a thinner body than my Syrian and Russian friends. I can squeeze through the tiniest gaps. Keep me in a cage that has glass or plastic sides or an old fish tank with a wire top. I can easily wriggle out through the gaps in wire cages. You can keep two brothers in one large cage, but it is easier to keep only one hamster in a cage. I eat the same food as other hamsters, but I usually eat more green food and vegetables than some of my relatives.

# A Note To Parents

The relationship between child and pet can be a special one. We hope this book will encourage young pet owners to care for their pets responsibly. Studies show that developing positive relationships with pets can contribute to a child's self-esteem and self-confidence.

It is essential to stress that parents also play a crucial role in pet care. Parents need to help children develop responsible behaviors and attitudes toward pets. Children may need supervision while handling pets and caring for them. Parents may need to remind their children that animals—like people—need to be treated with love and respect.

In addition to a happy and suitable home, all pets need

food, water, and exercise. Being a pet owner can be a costly and time-consuming experience. Before choosing a pet, be certain that your family's lifestyle is conducive to the type of pet you wish to own. Talk to a local veterinarian if you have questions.

Owning a pet can provide a wonderful opportunity for children to learn about responsibility, compassion, and friendship. We wish your child many years of happiness and fulfillment with his or her new pet!

# Acknowledgements

The author and publisher would like to thank the owners who generously allowed their pets to be photographed for this book, and the children who agreed to be models. Specifically, they would like to thank Harriet de Freitas, Florence Elphick, Kate Elsom – and Peanut, Chloe Anderson – and Cookie, Sacha Wadey – and Toffee, Caroline Gosden, Sophie King and Claire Watson of Brinsbury College, Adversane – and Damascus, Ivan and Hong. Thanks also to Denis Blades of Gattleys, Storrington, Steyning Pet Shop, Pet Stop, Billingshurst, Neil Martin and Annika Sumner of Washington Garden Center, Washington, Rolf C. Hagen (U.K.) Ltd., Christy Emblem at Interpet Ltd., and Farthings Veterinary Group, Billingshurst.

Thanks are due to the following photographers and picture libraries who kindly supplied photographs that are reproduced in this book.
Marc Henrie: 36, 44.
RSPCA Photolibrary: 9 bottom right (Angela Hampton), 18 (Angela Hampton), 28 (Angela Hampton), 34 (Tim Sambrook), 37 (Angela Hampton), 39 (Angela Hampton), 46 (Mike Lane).